# PIERRE AND LUCE

BY
ROMAIN ROLLAND

*Translated by*
CHARLES DE KAY

NEW YORK
HENRY HOLT AND COMPANY
1922

bW

R6475p

*Printed in U. S. A.*

# THE ISLE OF CALMS

*"Just as the Gulf Stream embraces the Sargasso Sea into which gradually drift the odds and ends that are carried away by the marine currents into the regions of calm, so does our aerial current surround a region where the air is still. It is called* THE ISLE OF CALMS.*"*

DURATION OF THE STORY

From Wednesday evening, January 30, to
Good Friday, May 29, 1918.

# PIERRE AND LUCE

PIERRE plunged into the subway. A
feverish, a brutal crowd. On his feet near
the door, closely pressed in a bank of human
bodies and sharing the heavy atmosphere
passing in and out of their mouths, he stared
without seeing them at the black and rumbling vaults over which flickered the shining
eyes of the train. The same heavy shadows
lay in his mind, the same gleams, hard and
tremulous. Suffocating in the raised collar
of his overcoat, his arms jammed against his
sides and his lips compressed, his forehead
damp with perspiration momentarily cooled
by a current from outside when the door

opened, he tried hard not to see, he tried not
to breathe, he tried not to live.    The heart
of this young fellow of eighteen, still almost
a child, was full of a dull despair.    Above
his head, above the shadows of these long
vaulted ways, of this rat-run through which
the monster of metal whirled, all swarming
with human masks—was Paris, the snow,
the cold January darkness, the nightmare of
life and of death—the war.

The war!    Four years ago it was, the war
had come to stay.    It had weighed heavily
on his adolescent years.    It had caught him
by surprise in that morally critical period
when the growing boy, disquieted by the
awakening of his feelings, discovers with a
shock the existence of blind, bestial, crush-
ing forces in life whose prey he is and that
without having asked to live at all.    And if
he happens to be delicate in character, tender
of heart and frail as to body in the way
Pierre was, he experiences a disgust and
horror which he does not dare confide to
others for all these brutalities, these nasti-
nesses, all this nonsense of fruitful and

devouring nature—this breeding sow that gobbles up her litter of pigs.

In every growing youth between sixteen and eighteen there is a bit of the soul of Hamlet. Don't ask him to understand the war! (All right for you men, who have had your fill!) He has all he can do to understand life and forgive its existence. As a rule he digs himself in with his dream and with the arts, until the time comes when he has got used to his incarnation, and the grub has achieved its agonizing passage from larva to winged insect. What a need he has for peace and meditation during these April days so full of the trouble of maturing life! But they come after him to the bottom of his burrow, look him up, drag him from the dark while still so tender in his new-made skin. They toss him into the raw air amongst the hard human race whose follies and hatreds he is expected at the very first moment to accept without understanding them and, not understanding, to atone for them.

Pierre had been called to military service

along with those of his own class, boys of sixteen to eighteen. Within six months his country would be needing his flesh. The war claimed him. Six months of respite. Six months! Oh, if one could only stop thinking at all from this time to that! Just to stay in this underground tunnel! Never see cruel daylight any more! . . .

He plunged deeper into his gloom along with the flying train and closed his eyes. . . .

When he opened them again—a few steps away, but separated by the bodies of two strangers, stood a young girl who had just entered. At first all he saw of her was a delicate profile under the shadow of her hat, one blonde curl on a somewhat thin cheek, a highlight perched upon the smooth cheekbone, the fine line of nose and lifted upper lip, and her mouth, slightly parted, still quivering a little from her sudden rush into the car. Through the portals of his eyes into his heart she entered, she entered all complete; and the door closed. Noises from without fell to nothing. Silence. Peace. She was there.

She did not look at him. In fact she did not even know as yet of his existence. And yet she was there inside him. He held her image there, speechless, crushed in his arms, and he dared not breathe for fear that his breath might ruffle her.

A jostling at the next station. Noisily talking, the crowd threw themselves into the already packed carriage. Pierre found himself shoved and carried along by the human wave. Above the tunnel vault, in the city up there, certain dull reports. The train started up again. At that moment a man quite out of his senses, who covered up his face with his hands, came running down the stairway of the station and rolled down on the floor at the bottom. There was just enough time to catch sight of the blood that trickled through his fingers. . . . Then the tunnel and darkness again. In the car frightened outcries: "The Gothas are at it again!" During the general excitement which fused these closely packed bodies into one, his hand had seized the hand that touched him.   And when he raised his eyes he saw it was She.

She did not pull her hand away.   At the pressure of his fingers hers replied in a sympathy of emotion, drawing together a bit, and then letting themselves go, soft and burning, without budging.   Thus the two remained in the protective darkness, their hands like two birds hid in the same nest; and the blood from their hearts ran in a single flood through the warmth of their palms.   They said no word to one another. His mouth almost touched the curl on her cheek and the tip of her ear.   They did not make a gesture.   She did not look at him. Two stations beyond, she loosed her hand from his, which did not keep her, slipped between the bodies and left without having looked at him.

When she had vanished it occurred to him to follow . . . Too late.   The train was in motion.   At the next stop he ran up to the surface.   There he found the nocturnal cold, the unseen touches of some flakes of snow and the City, frightened and amused at its fright; above it very high in the air circled the warlike birds. But he saw only her, the one who was within him; and he reached home holding the hand of the unknown girl.

PIERRE AUBIER lived with his parents near Cluny Square. His father was a municipal judge; his brother, older than he by six years, had volunteered at the beginning of the war. A good sound family of the *bourgeois* class, excellent folks, affectionate and human, never having dared to think for themselves and very probably never imagining that such a thing could be. Profoundly honest and with a lofty sense of the duties of his office, Judge Aubier would have rejected with indignation as a supreme insult the suspicion even that the verdicts he announced could have been dictated by any other considerations than those of equity and his own conscience. But the voice of his conscience had never spoken—let us better say whispered—against the government. For that conscience was born a functionary. It registered thoughts as a State function—

8

variable but infallible. Established powers
were invested by him with a sacred truth.
He admired sincerely those souls of iron, the
great free and unbending magistrates of the
past; and perhaps secretly believed himself
to be of their stock. He was a very small
edition of Michel de l' Hospital over whom
a century of republican slavery had passed.

As to Madame Aubier she was as good a
Christian as her husband was a good republican. Just as sincerely and honestly as he
made himself a docile instrument of the government against any form of liberty which
was not official, so did she mingle her pray-
ers, and that in perfect purity of heart, with
the homicidal vows which were made about
the war in every country of Europe by the
Catholic priests, the Protestant ministers, the
rabbis and the popes, the newspapers and the
right-minded thinkers of the time. And both
of them, father and mother, adored their
children and, like true French people, had
for them only a profound, essential affection,
would have sacrificed everything for them,
and yet, in order to do as others, would

sacrifice them without hesitation. To whom?
Why, to the unknown god. In every epoch
Abraham has led Isaac to the funeral pile.
And his magnificent folly still remains an
example for poor human beings.

As often is the case, at this family hearth
affection was great and intimacy null. How
should thoughts communicate freely from
one to the other when each one forbore a
look into the bottom of his own mind?
Whatever one may feel, one knows that certain dogmas at any rate must be blinked,
set aside; and if it already amounts to an
embarrassment when the dogmas are discreet
enough to stay within the limits traced for
them (that was the case, to sum all up, of
those belonging to the beyond) what is to be
said when they pretend to mix themselves
with life, to rule life entirely as our laical
and obligatory dogmas actually do? Just
you try to forget the dogma of your country!
The new religion compelled a return to the
Old Testament. It was not to be made com-
fortable with lip devotion and innocent
rituals, hygienic and ridiculous, like confes-

sion, Friday fasting, rest on Sunday, which
once upon a time incited the racy spirit of
our "philosophers" during the period when
the people were free—under the kings. The
new religion wanted all, was not satisfied
with less; all the man complete, his body,
his blood, his life and his thinking mind.
Above all his blood. Since the time of the
Aztecs of Mexico never was there a divinity
so gorged with blood. It would be deeply
unjust to say that the believers did not suffer
from this. They suffered, but they believed.
Alas my poor brother men, for whom suffering itself is a proof positive of the
divine! . . .

Mr. and Mrs. Aubier suffered like the
others, and like the others adored. But
from a growing boy one could not demand
such abnegation of heart, feeling and good
sense. Pierre would have liked to comprehend at least what it was that oppressed him.
What a lot of questions burned within which
he could not utter! For the very first word
of all was, "But what if I don't believe in it
at all!"—a blasphemy just to start with.

No, he could not speak out.    They would
have gazed at him in a stupor, frightened,
indignant—with sorrow and shame.    And
since he was at that plastic age when the soul,
with a bark still too tender, wrinkles up at
the slightest breeze that comes from outside
and under its furtive fingers molds its form
shudderingly, he felt himself beforehand
sorrowful and ashamed.    Ah!  how they
believed, all of them!   (But did they really
all of them believe?)    How was it they
managed it then?—One did not dare to ask.
Not to believe, standing all alone among all
those who do believe, is like one who lacks
some organ, superfluous perchance, but one
that all the others possess; and so, blushing,
one hides one's nudity from the public.

The only one who was able to comprehend
the tortures of the young fellow was his elder
brother.    Pierre had for Philip that adora-
tion which the younger ones often have (but
which they jealously conceal) for the older
brother or sister, some stranger comrade,
at times merely the vision of an hour and
lost again—who realizes in their eyes the

dream at once of what they could wish to be
and of what they would like to love: chaste
ardors and troublesome, of the future, formed
of mixing currents. The big brother was
aware of this naïve homage and was flat-
tered by it. Not so long ago he had tried
to read the heart of the little brother, and
explain things to him with discretion; for,
although more robust, like him he was
molded of that fine clay which, among the
better sort of men, retains a little of the
woman and does not blush to own it. But
the war had come and torn him away
from his hard working career, from his study
of the sciences, from his twenty-year-old
dream and from his intimacy with his
young brother. He had dropped everything
in the intoxicating idealism of the moment,
like a big crazy bird that launches out into
space with the heroic and absurd illusion
that his beak and his talons will put an end
to the war and restore to earth the reign of
peace. Since then the big bird had returned
two or three times to the nest; each time, alas,
a little more worn in plumage. He had

come back denuded of many of his illusions,
but he found himself too much mortified
about them to acknowledge it.    He was
ashamed to have believed in them.    Folly,
not to have known how to see life as it is!
Now he set his heart upon dissipating its
enchantment and accepting it stoically, what-
soever it might turn out.    Not himself alone
did he punish; a wretched suffering urged
him to punish his illusions in the heart of
his young brother, where he found that they
held their own.    At his first coming back,
when Pierre had run up to him burning in
his walled-up heart, he had been frozen at
once by the welcome his elder gave him,
affectionate certainly, always affectionate,
but with a certain harsh irony in his tone
hard to fathom.    Questions that pressed
forward to his lips were pushed back on the
instant.    Philip had seen them coming and
cut them down with a word, with a look.
After two or three attempts Pierre drew back
with an aching heart.    He did not recognize
his brother any more.    The other recognized
him only too well.    He perceived in him

what he himself had been not so long ago
and what never he could be again.    He
made him pay for it.    It caused him regret
afterward, but of that he showed no sign and
just began over again.    Both of them suffered and, through a too common misunder-
standing, their suffering, so much alike, so
near, which ought to have brought them
together, only separated them.    The sole
difference between them was that the elder
knew that it was near while Pierre believed
himself alone in his suffering with nobody
to whom he could open his soul.

Then why did he not turn toward those of
his own age, his companions at school?    It
might seem as if these growing youths ought
to have come close to one another and
mutually given one another support.    But
nothing of the kind.    On the contrary, a
sorrowful fatality kept them separate, scattered in little groups, and even in the inner
circle of these minim groups kept them
distant and reserved.    The commoner sort
had plunged, eyes closed, head foremost into
the current of the war.    The larger number

drew themselves away and did not feel any
connection with the generations that preceded
them; they did not partake in any way of
their passions, their hopes and their hatreds;
they were bystanders beside all the frantic
goings-on like men who are sober looking
on at those who are drunk.   But what could
they do in opposition?   Many had started
little magazines, reviews whose ephemeral
lives were snuffed out after the first numbers
for lack of air; the censorship produced a
vacuum; the entire thought of France was
under the pneumatic exhausting bell. Among
these young fellows the most distinguished
ones, too feeble to rebel and too proud to
complain, knew beforehand that they were
delivered up to the sword of war.   While
they waited for their turn at the slaughterhouse they looked on and made their judg-
ments in silence, each one by himself, with
a little surprise and a great deal of irony.
Through a disdainful reaction against the
mental condition of the herd they fell back
into a kind of egotism, intellectual and artis-
tic egotism, an idealistic sensualism, where

the tracked and hunted ego vindicated its rights against human fellowship. Laughable fellowship, which made itself manifest to these adolescents only in the shape of finished murder, one undergone in common! A precocious experience had shriveled their illusions: they had seen how much those same illusions were worth in their elders and how those who did not believe in them paid for them with their lives. Even as to those of their own age and as to man in general their confidence was shaken. And besides, at such a time it cost something to confide in people! Every day one learned of some denunciation of thoughts and intimate conversations by a patriotic spy whose zeal the government honored and stimulated. So it was that these young people, through discouragement, through disdain, through prudence, through a stoical sense of their solitude in thought, gave themselves very little indeed the one to the other.

Pierre could not find among them that Horatio whom little eighteen-year-old Hamlets seek. If he had a horror of estranging his thought from public opinion (that public woman) he did feel the need of joining it freely with souls of his own choosing. He was too tender to be able to content himself with himself. He suffered from the universal suffering. That crushed him by the amount of its pain, which he exaggerated:— for if humanity does support it in spite of everything, that is because humanity has a harder hide than is the delicate skin of a frail boy. But what he did not exaggerate and what weighed him down much more than the suffering of the world was the imbecility of it all.

It is nothing to undergo pain, it is nothing to die, if only one can see a reason for it. Sacrifice is a good thing when one understands why it is made. But what is this why? What is the sense of this world and its harrowings for a youth? If he be sincere and sound of mind, in what way can he interest himself in the coarse medley of nations standing head to head like stupid rams on the brink of an abyss, into which all are about to tumble? And yet the road was

broad enough for all.   Why then this mad-
ness to destroy oneself?   Why these countries given over to pride, these States devoted
to rapine, these peoples to whom is taught
murder, as if murder were their duty?   But
wherefore this butchery everywhere among
living beings?   Why this world that devours
itself?   To what purpose the nightmare of
that monstrous and endless chain of life,
each one of whose links sets its jaws into the
neck of the other, feasts on its flesh, delights
in its suffering and lives through its death?
Why the conflict and why the pain?   Why
death?   Why life?   Why?   Why? . . .

That night when the boy got home the
why had ceased its cry.

NEVERTHELESS nothing had changed. There he was in his own room littered with papers and books. All about the familiar sounds. In the street the trumpet sounding the close of the warning against airbombs. On the house stairs the reassured gossip of the tenants coming up from the cellar. In the story overhead the crazy marching to and fro of the old neighbor who for months had been waiting for his vanished son.

But here in his own chamber lay no longer those cares of his in ambush which he had left there. . . .

Sometimes it happens that an incomplete accord in music sounds raucous in a way; it leaves the mind disquieted, up to the moment when some note is added which procures a fusion of the hostile or coldly alien elements, like visitors who do not know one

another and wait to be introduced.    At once
the ice is broken and harmony spreads from
one member of the group to another.    This
moral chemistry had just been put in opera-
tion by a warm and furtive contact of hands.
Pierre was not conscious of the reason for the
change; he never dreamed of analyzing.
But he felt that the habitual hostility of
things in general had suddenly softened.
A shooting pain takes possession of your
head for hours; of a sudden you perceive it
is no longer there: how was it that it went?
Scarcely a feeling of buzzing about the
temples to recall it.  .  .  .   Pierre was a bit
suspicious of this new-found calm.    He
suspected that it concealed under a passing
truce a much worse return of the pain which
was merely taking breath.    Already was he
acquainted with the respites that are ob-
tained through the arts.   When into our
eyes penetrate the divine proportions of lines
and colors, or into the voluptuous windings
of the sonorous ear-shell the lovely, varied
play of accords which combine and interlock
in obedience to the laws of harmonious num-

bers, peace takes possession of us and joy
inundates our souls. But that is a radiance
which comes from outside; one would say
from a sun, the distant fires of which hold
us in suspense fascinated, lifted high above
our life. It endures only a moment and
then one falls again. Art is never more
than a passing forgetfulness of the actual,
the real. Pierre was afraid and fully expected the same deception.—But this time the
radiation came from within. Nothing that
belongs to life was forgot. But everything
fell into harmony. His recollections, his
new thoughts. Even to the familiar objects
about him: the books and papers in his
chamber sprang alive and took on an interest
which they had lost.

For months past his intellectual growth
had been compressed like a young tree which
is struck in full blossoming by the "saints of
the ice." He did not belong to those practical boys who profit by the indulgence
offered at universities to the younger classes
just about to be called to the colors in order
to pull out hastily a diploma from under the

indulgent eyes of the examiners.   Nor was
he one to feel the despairing eagerness of the
young man who sees death approaching and
so takes double mouthfuls and devours the
arts and sciences which he will never have
a chance to test and verify in life.    That
perpetual feeling of emptiness at the end,
emptiness that is underneath and everywhere
hidden beneath the cruel and absurd illusion
of the world—this it was that swept aside
all his enthusiasms.    He would throw
himself on a book, on a thought—then 'he
stopped, discouraged.    Whither would that
lead?   What the use of learning?   What is
the point of getting riches if it be necessary
to lose everything, leave everything, if
nothing really belongs to you?    In order
that activity, in order that science should
have any sense, it is necessary that life
should have some.    This sense no effort of
the mind, no supplication from the heart had
been able to produce for him.—And yet, lo
and behold, all of itself, this sense had
come. . . .   Life had some sense. . . .
What then?—And seeking to find whence

came this inner smile—he beheld the parted lips upon which his mouth was burning to press itself.

In ordinary times, no doubt, this wordless fascination would not have persisted. At that period of upgrowth when one is a lover of love, one sees love in every eye; the greedy and uncertain heart gathers it flitting from one to the other, and nothing forces it to settle down; the heart is just beginning its day.

But the day at the present period will be a short one: it is necessary to hurry up.

The heart of this young fellow was in a hurry all the greater because it was so much behindhand. Great cities which from a distance appear like the smoking solfataras of sensuality really harbor fresh souls and ingenuous bodies. How many young men and young girls there are who respect love and keep their senses virgin up to the marriage day! Even in the refined circles where mental curiosity is precociously excited, what

singular ignorances conceal themselves under
the free talk of some young worldly girl or of
some student who knows everything and
understands nothing! In the heart of Paris
there are provinces most naïve, little gardens
as of cloisters, pure existences as of springs.
Paris permits herself to be betrayed by her
literature. Those who speak in her name
are the most soiled of all. And besides, one
only knows too well that a false human
consideration often prevents the pure from
avowing their innocence.—Pierre did not yet
understand love; and he was delivered up to
the first appeal love made.

This also added to the enchantment of his
thought: that love had been born under the
wing of death. In that moment of emotion
when they felt the menace of the bombs pass
over their heads, when the bloodstained
apparition of the wounded man contracted
their hearts, then it was their fingers groped
toward each other; and both of them had
read therein, at the same time with the
quivering of the flesh that was frightened,
the loving consolation of an unknown

friend.    Fleeting pressure!    One of the two
hands, that of the man, says: "Lean upon
me!"      And the other, the maternal one,
pushes aside her own fear in order to say:
"My little dear!"

Nothing of all this was uttered or heard.
But that inward murmur filled the soul far
better than words, that curtain of foliage
which masks our thought.    Pierre allowed
himself to be cradled by this humming.
Such the song of a golden wasp that floats
through the chiaroscuro of one's thought.
His days became numb things in this new
languor.    That solitary and naked heart
dreamed of the warmth of a nest.

During these first weeks of February,
Paris was counting her ruins from the last
raid and licking her wounds.    The press,
locked up in its kennel, was barking for
reprisals.    And, according to the statement
of "the Man who put the fetters on," the
government was making war on the French.
The open season for suits at law for treason-
able acts commenced.    The spectacle of a
wretched creature who was defending his

own head, bitterly demanded by the public
accuser, was a matter of amusement for
*Tout-Paris,* whose appetite for the theatre
had not yet been satisfied by four years of
war and ten millions of dead men dissolving
behind the flies.

But the youth remained completely and
solely absorbed in the mysterious guest who
had just come to make him a visit.  Strange
intensity of these visions of love printed on
the very floor of his thought and nevertheless
lacking in contour!  Pierre would have
been incapable of saying what was the form
of her features or what the color of her
eyes or the modeling of her lips.  All he
could bring back was the emotion already in
himself.  All his attempts to give precision
to the image merely ended in deforming it.
He was no more successful when he went to
work to find her in the streets of Paris.  At
every turn he believed he had seen her.  It
was either a smile or a white young neck or
a gleam in some eyes.  And then the blood
shook in his heart.  There was no resem-
blance, none whatever, between these flying

images and the real image which he sought
and which he believed he loved. Well, then,
he did not love her? Surely he loved her;
and that is why he saw her everywhere and
under every shape. For she just is every
smile, each radiance, all life. And the exact
form would be a limitation.—But one longs
for that limitation in order to clasp love and
to possess it.

Though he might never see her again he
knew that she existed, she existed, and that
she was the nest. In the hurricane a port.
A lighthouse in the night. *Stella Maris,
Amor.* Oh, Love, watch over us at the hour
of death! . . .

ALONG the quay of the Seine beside the Institute he wandered, looking with little attention at the shelves of the few *bouquinistes* who had stuck to their posts. He found himself at the foot of the steps of the Pont des Arts. Raising his eyes he perceived her for whom he had waited. A portfolio of drawings under her arm, she came down the steps like a little doe. He did not reflect for the shadow of a second; he rushed forward to meet her and while he ascended toward her who was coming down, for the first time their gaze rested the one on the other and entered. Arrived in front of her and stopping short, he began to blush. Surprised, seeing that he blushed, she reddened too. Before he could get his breath again the little deerlike step had already gone beyond him. When strength returned and he was able to turn about her skirt was dis-

appearing at the turning of the arcáde which
looks upon the Rue de Seine. He did not
try to follow her. Leaning against the
balustrade of the bridge, he saw *her own*
look in the stream that flowed below. For
some time his heart had a pasture new. . . .
(Oh, dear, stupid children!) . . .

A week later he was loafing in the Luxembourg Gardens which the sun was filling
with a golden softness. Such a radiant
February in that funereal year! Dreaming
with his eyes open and hardly knowing well
whether he was dreaming what he saw, or
saw what he was dreaming, steeped in a
greedy languor obscurely happy, unhappy, in
love, as much filled full of tenderness as with
the sun, he smiled as he strolled with inattentive eyes, and without his knowing it his lips
moved, reciting words without connection, a
song of some kind. He looked down at the
sandy path and, like the wingtip of a dove
that passes, he had an impression that a smile
had just passed along. He whirled about
and saw that he had just crossed her path.
And just at that moment, without stopping in

her walk, she turned her head with a smile in order to observe him. Then he hesitated no longer and went toward her, his hands almost extended in so juvenile and naïve a rush that naïvely she waited for him. He made no excuses for himself. There was no awkwardness between them. It seemed to them they were continuing an interview already begun.

"You are laughing at me," said he; "you are quite right!"

"I'm not laughing at you"—(her voice like her step was lively and supple)—"you were laughing all to yourself; I merely laughed at seeing you."

"Was I laughing, really?"

"You are still laughing now."

"Now I know why."

She did not ask him what he meant. They walked side by side. They were happy.

"What a jolly little sun!" said she.

"Newly born springtide!"

"Was it to him just now you were sending that little smile?"

"Not to him alone.    Perhaps to you, too."

"Little liar!    Bad boy.    You don't even know me."

"As if one could say such a thing!    We have seen each other I don't know how often!"

"Thrice, counting this time."

"Ah—you remember, then?    You see that we are old acquaintances!"

"Let's talk about it."

"I'm agreed.    That's all I want!  .  .  . Oh, come, let us sit there!    Just an instant, won't you please?    It's so nice at the edge of the water!"

(They were near the Galathea Fountain, which the masons had covered over with tarpaulins to protect it from the bombs.)

"I really can not, I shall miss my train."

She gave him the hour.    He showed her that she had more than twenty-five minutes.

Yes, but she wanted first to buy her lunch at the corner of Rue Racine, where they keep good little buns.    He hauled one out of his pocket.

"Oh, forgive me! . . . But how were you able to see?"

She did not answer; but in that mocking profile he could see the corner of her eye and that was laughing.

"Oh, you slyboots!"

"It's very simple. Everybody can do that."

"I never could."

"Just try. . . . You simply squint."

"I never could, never. In order to see it's necessary for me to look right to the front, stupidly."

"Oh, no, not so stupidly!"

"At last! I see your eyes."

They looked at each other, gently laughing.

"What's your name?"

"Luce."

"That's a lovely name, lovely as this day!"

"And yours?"

"Pierre—rather worn out."

"A fine name—that has honest and clear eyes."

"Like mine."

"Well, yes, so far as clear goes they are."

"That's because they're looking at Luce."

"Luce? . . . People say 'Mademoi-selle.' "

"No."

"No?"

(He shook his head.)

"You are not 'Mademoiselle.' You are just Luce and I am Pierre."

They were holding hands; and without looking at one another, their eyes fixed upon the tender blue of the sky between the branches of the leafless trees, they kept silence. The flood of their thoughts inter-mingled by way of their hands.

She said:

"The other night both of us were afraid."

"Yes," said he, "how good it was."

(Only later they smiled at having ex-pressed, each one, what the other was dream-ing of.)

She tore her hand away and suddenly sprang up, having heard the clock strike.

"Oh, I have scarcely more than time left . . ."

Together they marched at that little quick-step the Parisian women take so prettily, so that seeing them trot, one scarcely thinks of their swiftness, so easy appears the gait.

"Do you pass here often?"

"Every day.   But oftener on the other side of the terrace."   (She pointed to the garden with its Watteau trees.)   "I am just back from the Museum."

(He looked at the portfolio she carried.)

"Painter?" he asked.

"No," she replied, "that's too big a word. A little dauberette."

"Why?   For your own pleasure?"

"Oh, no indeed!   For money."

"For money?"

"It's horrid, isn't it?  to make art for money?"

"It's particularly astonishing to make money if one cannot paint."

"It's just for that reason, you see.   I'll explain it to you another time."

"Another time, by the fountain, we'll have lunch again."

"We shall see. If it's good weather."

"But you will come earlier? Will you not? Say yes . . . Luce . . ."

(They were come to the station. She jumped on the running board of the tram car.)

"Answer, say yes, little light! . . ."

She did not answer; but when the tram was in motion she made a "yes" with her eyelids and he read on her lips without her having spoken:

"Yes, Pierre."

Both of them thought, as they went their way:

"It's amazing, this evening, what a happy look everybody has!"

And they kept smiling without taking heed of what had occurred. They knew only that they had *it,* that they possessed *it* and that *it belonged* to them. It? What? Nothing. We feel rich this evening! . . . On getting home they looked at themselves carefully in the mirror just as one looks at a friend, with loving eyes.    They said to themselves: "That gaze of his, of hers, was fixed on *you*."    They went to bed early, overcome—but wherefore?—by a delicious weariness.    While they undressed they kept thinking:

"What's best of all at present is, that there's a tomorrow."

TOMORROW! . . . Those who come after us will have some difficulty in understanding what silent despair and weariness of spirit without grounds that word evoked during the fourth year of the war. . . . Oh, such a weariness! So many times had hopes been destroyed! Hundreds of tomorrows just like yesterday and today followed on, each similarly devoted to emptiness and waiting—to waiting for emptiness. Time no longer ran. The year was like a river Styx which encircles life with the circuit of its black and greasy waters, with its somber, watery, silky flood that seems no longer to move. Tomorrow? Tomorrow is dead.

In the hearts of these children Tomorrow was resuscitated from the grave.

Tomorrow saw them seated again near the fountain. And tomorrows followed one another. The fine weather favored these

very brief meetings, every day a little less
brief. Each one brought a lunch in order
to have the pleasure of exchanging. Pierre
now waited at the door of the Museum. He
wanted to see her art works. Although she
was not proud of them she did not make him
beg at all before showing them. They were
reproductions of famous paintings in miniature, or portions of paintings, a group, a
figure, a bust. Not too disagreeable at the
first glance but extremely loose in drawing.
Here and there quite true and pretty touches;
but right alongside the mistakes of a pupil,
exhibiting not merely the most elementary
ignorance but a reckless ease perfectly careless of what anyone might think.—"Enough!
Good enough the way they are!"—Luce
recited the names of the pictures copied.
Pierre knew them too well. His face was
quite drawn from his discomfiture. Luce
felt that he was not pleased; but she sum-
moned all her courage to show him everything—and this one too. . . . Woof!
. . . it was the ugliest one she had! ?
She kept up her mocking smile which was

directed to her own address as well as to
Pierre's; but she would not confess to herself a pinch of vexation. Pierre hardened
his lips in order not to speak. But at last it
was too much for him. She showed him a
copy of a Florentine Raphael.

"But these are not its colors!" said he.

"Oh, well, that wouldn't be surprising,"
said she. "I didn't go and look at it. I took
a photo."

"And didn't anybody object?"

"Who? My clients? They haven't been
to look at it either. . . . And besides, even
if they had seen it, they don't look so nar-
rowly! The red, the green, the blue—they
only see the fire in it. Sometimes I copy the
original in colors, but I change the colors.
. . . See here, for instance, this one . . ."
(An angel by Murillo).

"Do you find it's better?"

"No, but it amused me. . . . And then,
it's easier. . . . And besides, it's all the
same to me. The essential thing is that this
will sell. . . ."

At this last piece of boasting she stopped,

took the color sketches from him and burst
out laughing.

"Ha! So they're even uglier than you
had expected?"

He said, greatly annoyed:

"But why, why do you make things like
these?"

She examined his upset visage with a
kindly smile of maternal irony; this dear
little *bourgeois* for whom everything had
been so easy and who could not conceive that
one must make concessions for . . .

He asked once more:

"Why? Tell me, why?"

(He was quite crestfallen, as if it was he
who was the botcher in paint! . . . Dear
little boy! She would have liked to kiss
him . . . very properly, on his forehead!)

She answered gently:

"Why, in order to live."

He was quite overcome. He had never
dreamed of it.

"Life is complicated," she went on in a
light and mocking tone. "In the first place

it is necessary to eat, and then to eat every day. In the evening one has dined. It's necessary to begin again the next day. And then it's necessary to dress oneself. Dress oneself completely, body, head, hands, feet. That's so far as clothing is concerned! And then pay for it all. For everything. Life, it's just paying."

For the first time he saw what had escaped the shortsightedness of his love: the modest fur in some places worn, the shoes somewhat the worse for wear, the traces of embarrassed means which the natural elegance of a little Parisian woman makes one forget. And his heart contracted within him.

"Ah! couldn't I be allowed, couldn't I be permitted to help you?"

She moved away from him a bit and reddened:

"No, no," she returned, much upset, "there's no question of that. . . . Never! . . . I have no need . . ."

"But it would make me so happy!"

"No. . . . Nothing more to be said

about that.    Or we shall not be friends any
more  .  .  ."

"We are friends, then?"

"Yes.  That's to say, if you are so still
after you have seen these horrible daubs?"

"Surely, surely!    It isn't your fault."

"But do they trouble you?"

"Oh, yes."

She laughed out contentedly.

"That makes you laugh, naughty girl!"

"No, it's not being naughty.    You do not
understand."

"Then why do you laugh?"

"I shan't tell you."

(She was thinking: "Love! how kind you
are to be troubled because I have done something that is ugly!")

She went on:

"You are so kind.    Thank you."

(He looked at her with astonished eyes.)

"Don't try to understand," said she, tap-
ping him softly on his hand.  .  .  .  "There,
let's talk of something else.  .  .  ."

"Yes.    But one word more.  .  .  .  Still,
I could wish to know.  .  .  .  Tell me (and

don't be hurt) . . . Are you at the present moment a bit strapped?"

"No, no, I told you that just now, because there have been now and then hard times. But now it goes much better. Mama has found a situation where she is well paid."

"Your mother is at work?"

"Yes, in a munitions factory. She gets twelve francs a day. It's a fortune."

"In a factory! A war factory!"

"Yes."

"Why, it's frightful!"

"Oh, well! One takes what offers!"

"Luce! but if you, you should have such an offer? . . ."

"Oh, me? You see yourself, I just daub. Ah! You perceive now that I have good reason to make my smears!"

"But if it were necessary to have money and there were no other way than to work in one of those factories that produce bomb-shells, would you go?"

"If it were necessary to make money and no other means? . . . Why, surely! I would run for it."

"Luce! Do you realize what it is they're doing in there?"

"No, I don't think about it."

"Everything that will make people suffer, die, that tears them to pieces, that burns, that tortures beings like you, like me . . ."

She put her hand on her mouth to signal to him to hush.

"I know, I know all that, but I don't want to think of it."

"You don't want to think about it?"

"No," said she.

And a moment after:

"One must live. . . . If one thinks about it, one cannot live any more. For myself I want to live, I want to live. If they compel me to do that in order to live, shall I torment myself on this account or on that? That's no business of mine; it isn't I that wants it. If it is wrong it is not my fault, not my own. As for me, what I want is nothing bad."

"And what is it you do want?"

"First of all I want to live."

"You love life?"

"Why, of course. Am I wrong in that?"

"Oh, no! It is so jolly that you do live. . . ."

"And you, you don't love it also?"

"I did not, up to the time . . ."

"Up to the time?"

(This question did not call for an answer. Both of them knew it.)

Following up his thought, Pierre:

"You just said 'first of all.' . . . 'I want to live, first of all.' . . . And what then? What else do you wish?"

"I don't know."

"Yes, you do know . . ."

"You are very indiscreet."

"Yes, very."

"It embarrasses me to tell you . . ."

"Tell me in my ear. No one will overhear."

She smiled:

"I would like . . ." (she hesitated).

"I would like just *a little bit* of happiness . . ."

(They were quite close the one to the other.)

She went on:

"Is that too much to ask? . . . They have often told me that I'm an egotist; and as for me, I sometimes say to myself: What has one a right to?   When one sees so many wretchednesses, so much pain about one, you hardly dare to ask. . . . But in spite of all my heart does insist and cries out: Yes, I have the right, I have the right to a very little portion of happiness . . . Tell me very frankly, is that being an egotist?   Do you think that wrong?"

He was overcome by an infinite pity. That cry of the heart, that poor little naïve cry stirred him down to his soul.   Tears came to his eyes.   Side by side on the bench, leaning one against the other, they felt the warmth of their legs.   He would have liked to turn toward her and take her in his arms. He did not dare move for fear of not remaining in control of his emotion.   Immovable, they looked straight forward at the ground before their feet.   Very swiftly, in a low ardent voice, almost without moving his lips, he said:

"Oh, my darling little body! Oh, my heart! Would I could hold your little feet in my hands, upon my mouth. . . . I would like to eat you all . . ."

Without budging and very low and very quickly, just as he had spoken, she replied full of trouble: "Crazy! Foolish boy! Silence! I beg of you . . ."

A stroller-by of a certain age limped slowly past them. They felt their two bodies melt together with tenderness. . . .

Nobody left on the walk. A sparrow with ruffled feathers was dusting itself in the sand. The fountain shed its lucent droplets. Timidly their faces turned one toward the other; and scarcely had their eyes met each other, when like the rush of birds their mouths met, frightened and closely pressed—and then they flew apart. Luce sprang up, departed. He also had risen. She said to him: "Stay here."

They did not dare to look at one another any longer. He murmured:

"Luce! That little bit . . . that little bit of happiness . . . say, now we have it!"

THE weather caused an interruption to the lunches by the fountain of the sparrows. Fogs came to obscure the February sun. But they could not snuff out the one they carried in their hearts. Ah! all the bad weather you could wish might be on hand: cold, hot, rain, wind, snow or sun! Everything would be well, always. And even, things would be better. For when happiness is in its period of growth the very finest of all the days is always today.

The fog offered them a benevolent pretext not to separate during a portion of the day. Less risk that way of being observed. In the morning he went to wait for her at the arrival of the train and he accompanied her in her walks about Paris. He had the collar of his overcoat turned up. She wore a fur toque, her boa rolled in a chilly way up to her chin, her little veil

tightly tied on, which her lips pushed out
and made in it a small round relief. But
the best veil was the moist network of the
protective mist. The mist was like a curtain
of ashes, dense, grayish, with phosphorescent
spots. One could not see farther than ten
yards. It became thicker and thicker as they
passed down the old streets perpendicular to
the Seine. Friendly fog, in which a dream
stretches itself between ice-cold linen and
shudders with delight! They were like the
almond in the shell of the nut, like a flame
enclosed in a dark lantern. Pierre held the
left arm of Luce closely pressed to him;
they walked with the same step, almost of the
same stature, she a trifle taller, twittering in
a halfvoice, their figures quite close together;
he would have liked to kiss the little moist
round on her veil.

She was going to the shopman who sold
"false antiques"—who had ordered them—
to dispose of her "turnips," her "little beets"
as she called them. They were never in a
great hurry to reach the place and without
doing so on purpose (at least that is what

they insisted) took the longest way about,
putting their mistake to the debit of the fog.
When at last, nevertheless, the place came to
meet them despite all the efforts made to get
it off the track, Pierre stayed at a distance.
She entered the shop. He waited at the
corner of the street. He waited a long time
and he was not very warm. But he was glad
to wait and not to be warm and even to be
bored, because it was all for her. At last she
came out again and quick, quick she skipped
up to him, smiling, tender, in great disquiet
lest he be frozen. He saw in her eyes when
she had succeeded and then he rejoiced over
it as if it were he who had made the money.
But most often she came back to him empty
handed; it was necessary to return to the
shop two or three days in succession in order
to obtain her pay. Very happy she, if they
did not give her back the object ordered
accompanied by rebukes! Today for instance they had made a great fuss on account
of a miniature painted from the photograph
of an honest fellow deceased, whom she had
never seen. The family was indignant

because she had not given him the exact
colors of his eyes and hair.    It was necessary
to do it all over again.    Since she was dis-
posed rather to look at the comic side of her
misadventures, she laughed courageously
about it.    But Pierre did not laugh.    He
was furious.

"Idiots!    Triple idiots!"

When Luce showed him the photographs
which she had to copy in colors he thundered
in his disdain (Oh, how amused she was at
his comical fury!) at these heads of imbe-
ciles, frozen in solemn smiles.    That the
dear eyes of his Luce should have to apply
themselves to reproducing and her hands to
tracing the pictures of these mugs seemed to
him a profanation.    No, it was too revolt-
ing!    Copies from the museums were more
worth while.    But one could not count on
them any more.    The last museums had shut
their doors and no longer interested her
clients.    It was no longer the hour for Virgin
Maries and angels, only for the *poilus*.
Every family had its own, dead or alive,
oftener dead, and wanted to eternalize his

features. The wealthier ones wanted colors:
work paid for well enough, but beginning to
be scarce; it was needful for her not to be
capricious.    Lacking which, all that remained for the time being was the enlarging
of photographs at laughable prices.

The clearest point in all of this was that
she no longer had any reason to spend her
time in Paris: no more copies in the museum;
all that was needed being, to go to the shop
to collect and bring back the orders every two
or three days; the work itself could be done
at home.    That was not exactly what the two
children liked.    They continued to stroll
about the streets, unable to decide on taking
up the way to the station.    Since they felt
weary and the icy fog pierced them through,
they went into a church; and there, seated
most properly in the corner of a chapel, they
talked in low voices about the little common-
place affairs of their life while they looked at
the stained-glass windows.    From time to
time there fell a silence; and their souls, delivered from mere words (it was not the
meaning in the words that interested them

but their breath of life, like the furtive con-
tacts between quivering antennae) their souls
pursued another dialogue more solemn and
profound. The dreams in the colored
windows, the shadows cast by the piers, the
droning of the hymns mingled with their
dream, evoked the sorrowful facts of life
which they desired to forget and the consoling homesickness of the infinite. Although
it was nearly eleven o'clock, a yellowish twilight brimmed the nave like the oil of a
sacred cruet. From on high and from a
great distance came strange gleams, the
sombre purple of a window, a red pool on
violet ones, indistinct figures encircled by
their black settings. Against the high wall
of night the blood-like gleam of light made
a wound. . . .

Abruptly Luce remarked:

"Shall you have to be *taken?*"

He understood at once what she meant
for in the silence his spirit too had pursued
the same obscure trail.

"Yes," he said. "We mustn't talk of it."

"Only one thing. Tell me when?"

He told her:

"In six months."

She sighed.

He said:

"We mustn't think of it any more. What use would it be?"

She said:

"Yes, what use?"

They drew long breaths in order to push back the thought. Then courageously (or should one say to the contrary "timorously"? Let him who knows decide where true courage lies!) they both compelled themselves to talk of something else—of the stars of the candles, trembling in a reek, of the organ playing a prelude. Of the beadle who was passing. Of the box full of surprises which her handbag was, in which the indiscreet fingers of Pierre were rummaging. They had a very passion of amusing themselves with nothings. Neither one nor the other of these poor little creatures so much as considered the shadow of an idea of escaping from that destiny which must separate them. To make any resistance against the war, to

brave the current of a nation: as well to lift
up the church which covered them with its
shell! The only recourse was to forget, to
forget up to the last second, while hoping at
bottom that this last second would never
arrive. Until then, to be happy.

After they went out, while chatting, she
pulled him by the arm in order to cast a
glance at a shopfront, which they had just
passed. A shoe shop. He found his gaze
caressing tenderly a pair of fine leather
shoes, tall and laced up.

"Pretty, eh?" said he.

She said:

"A love!"

He laughed at the expression and she
laughed also.

"Wouldn't they be too big?"

"No, just a fit."

"Well, then, suppose one bought them?"

She pressed his arm and pulled him on so
as to tear him away from the sight.

"One has to belong to the wealthy"
(humming the air of *Dansons la capucine*.
. . .) "But they're not for us."

"Why not? Cinderella put the slipper on all right!"

"At that time there were fairies still."

"In the present time there are lovers still." She sang:

"*Non, non, nenni, mon petit ami!*"

"Why so, since we are friends?"

"Just for that reason."

"For that?"

"Yes, because one cannot accept things from a friend."

"Then perhaps—from an enemy?"

"Rather from a stranger; my shopman, for instance, if he wanted to advance me a payment, the robber!"

"But, Luce, I certainly have the right to order from you a painting, if I wish?"

She stopped, to burst out laughing.

"You, a painting by me? My poor friend, what could you do with it? You have gained a good deal of merit already, just for having looked at them. I know well enough that they are *croûtes*. They would stick in your throat."

"Not at all! Some of them are very

cunning.  And besides, if they suit my taste?"

"It's certainly changed since yesterday."

"Isn't it allowable to change one's taste?"

"No, not when one's a friend."

"Luce, do my portrait!"

"Well, well, now; his portrait!"

"Why, it's very serious.  I'm as good as those idiots . . ."

She squeezed his arm in an unthinking burst:

"Darling!"

"What was that you said?"

"I didn't say anything."

"I heard you all right."

"Well then, keep it for yourself!"

"No, I shan't keep it.  I'll give it back to you double. . . . Darling! . . . Darling!  You'll do my portrait, won't you? It's settled?"

"Have you a photo?"

"No, I have not."

"Then what do you expect?  I can't paint you in the street, I suppose."

"You told me that at home you were alone almost every day."

"Yes, the days mama works at the factory. . . . But I don't dare . . ."

"You are afraid, then, that we shall be seen?"

"No, that's not the reason. We have no neighbors."

"Well, then, what is it you're afraid of?"

She did not reply.

They were come to the square before the tramway station. Although all about them were people who were waiting, they were hardly to be seen, the fog continued to isolate the little couple. She evaded his eyes. He took her two hands and said tenderly:

"My darling, don't be afraid . . ."

She lifted her eyes and they gazed at each other. Their eyes were so loyal!

"I trust you," said she.

She closed her eyes. She felt that she was sacred to him.

They let go hands. The tram was about to start. Pierre's gaze questioned Luce.

"What day?" he demanded.

"Thursday," she replied. "Come about two."

At the moment of parting she regained her roguish smile; she whispered in his ear:

"And you must bring your photo just the same. I am not strong enough to paint without the photo. . . . Yes, yes, I know you have some, you naughty little humbug."

OUT beyond the Malakoff. Streets like broken teeth separated by vague regions losing themselves in a dubious kind of country-side where among boarded enclosures blossom the cabins of ragpickers. The gray dull sky is lying low over the colorless ground whose thin edges smoke with the fog. The air is chill. The house easy to find: there are only three of them on one side of the road. The last of the three; it has no neighbor across the street. It has but one story with a little courtyard which is surrounded by a picket fence; two or three starveling trees, a square patch of kitchen garden under the snow.

Pierre has made no noise on entering; the snow deadens his steps. But the curtains of the ground floor are in motion; and when he reaches the door, the door opens and Luce is on the threshold. In the half light of the

hall they say good day in a choking voice,
and she ushers him into the first apartment
which serves as dining-room. There it is
that she works: her easel is installed near
the window. At first they do not know what
to say to one another: both have thought
over this visit altogether too much beforehand; none of the speeches they had pre-
pared is able to come forth; and they talk
in a halfvoice, although there is nobody else
in the house—and it's just for that reason.
They stay seated at some distance from each
other with their arms rigid; and he has not
even thrown back the collar of his cloak.
They chat about the cold weather and the
hours of the tramcars. They are unhappy
to feel themselves so silly.

At last she makes an effort and asks if he
has brought the photographs, and scarcely
has he taken them from his pocket when both
pluck up a spirit. These pictures are the
intermediaries over whose heads the chat
revives; for now the two are not entirely
alone; there are eyes that look at you and
they are not embarrassing. Pierre has had

the clever idea (there was really no roguish-
ness in it) to bring all his photographs, from
the age of three; there was one that showed
him in a little skirt.    Luce laughed with
pleasure; she spoke to the photo in comical
baby talk.    Can there be anything more
delightful to a woman than to see the picture
of the person she loves when he was quite
small?    She cradles, she rocks him in her
thoughts, she gives him the breast; and she
is even not so far from the dream that she
has given him birth.    And besides (nor does
she dupe herself at all) it forms a convenient
pretext to say to the infant what she cannot
force herself to say to the grown-up.—When
he asks which one of the photographs she
prefers, she says without hesitating:

"The dear little codger  .  .  ."

How serious he looks, already!  Almost
more serious than today.  Certainly if Luce
dared to look (and just here she does dare)
in order to make comparisons with the
Pierre of today, she would see in his eyes
an expression of joy and infantile gayety
that does not appear in the infant: for the

eyes of this infant, this little *bourgeois*
under a bell glass, are birds in a cage that
lack sunlight; and the sunlight has come,
hasn't it, Luce?  .  .  .

In his turn he asks to see photos of Luce.
She exhibits a little girl of six with a big
plait who is squeezing a little dog in her
arms; and as she sees it again she thinks
mischievously that in that period she loved no
less fervently nor very differently; whatever
heart she possessed she gave it even then to
her dog; it was Pierre already, while waiting till he arrived.  Also she showed a young
miss of thirteen or fourteen who twisted her
neck with a coquettish and a somewhat pre-
tentious air; luckily there was always there
at the corners of the mouth that roguish little
smile which appeared to say:

"You know, I'm just amusing myself; I
don't take myself seriously."

Now they had completely forgotten their
former embarrassment.

She set herself to sketching-in the portrait.
Since he must not budge one bit any more,
nor talk except with the tips of his lips, she it

was who made almost all the conversation, all by herself. Instinct told her that silence was dangerous. And as it happens with sincere persons who talk at some length, she came quickly to the point of confiding to him the intimate affairs of her life and those of her family which she did not have the slightest intention of recounting. She heard herself speak with astonishment; but there was no way of returning to solid ground; the very silence of Pierre was like a declivity down which the stream glided. . . .

She recited the facts of her infant life in the provinces. She came from Touraine. Her mother belonging to a well-to-do family of the solid *bourgeoisie* became infatuated with a tutor, the son of a farmer. The *bourgeois* family opposed the marriage; but the two lovers were obstinate; the young girl had waited until she was of age in order to send out the legal summons to her family. After the marriage her people would not recognize her. The young couple lived through years of affection and hard fare. The husband wore himself out at his task and sickness arrived. The wife accepted this further burden courageously; she worked for two. Her parents, obstinately cherishing their wounded pride, refused to do anything to come to his assistance. The sick man died a few months before the outbreak of the war. And the two women did not try to renew connection with the mother's family. The latter would have welcomed the young girl if she had made any advances; she would have been received like a *mea culpa* condoning the action of her mother. But the family might wait! Rather eat stones for breakfast!

Pierre was amazed at the hard heartedness of these *bourgeois* parents. Luce did not find it extraordinary.

"Don't you believe there are a great many people like that? Not wicked. No, I am sure that my grandparents are not, and even believe that it pained them not to say to us: 'Come back!' But their self-respect had been mortified too much. And self-love among these people, there's nothing else that is so great. It is stronger than all the rest.

When one has done them wrong it is not merely the wrong that one has done them; there is *the Wrong;* the others are wrong and they themselves are right. And so, without being cruel (no, really, they are not) they would let you die near them at a slow fire rather than concede that perhaps after all they were not right. Oh, they are not the only ones! One meets with many others! . . . Say, am I mistaken? Aren't they just like that?"

Pierre pondered. He was excited. For he was thinking:

"Why, yes. That is the way they are. . . ."

Through the eyes of the little girl he saw abruptly the penury of heart, the desert-like aridity of this *bourgeois* class of which he formed a part. Dry and wornout earth which little by little has imbibed all the juices of life and does not renew them any more, just like those lands in Asia where the fecundating rivers, drop by drop, have disappeared under the vitreous sand. Even those whom they believe they love are loved in a proprietary way; they sacrifice them to their egotism, to their buttressed pride, to their narrow and headstrong intelligence. Pierre took a sorrowful review of his parents and himself. He was silent. The panes of the apartment vibrated under the shock of a distant cannonade. And Pierre, who was thinking of those who were dying, said with bitterness:

"And that, too, is their work."

Yes, the hoarse barking of these cannon away off there, the universal war, the grand catastrophe—the dryness of heart and the inhumanity of that braggart and limited *bourgeoisie* had a large part in the responsibility for all that. And now (which was only just) the unchained monster would never stop until it had devoured them.

And Luce said:

"That is true."

For without knowing that she did so she followed the thought of Pierre. He started at the echo:

"Yes, it is true," said he, "what has come

about is just. This world was too old; it ought to, it must die."

And Luce, bowing her head, sorrowful and resigned, said once more:

"Yes."

Solemn faces of children bent beneath Destiny, whose youthful brows touched by the wing of care bore within them such distressful ponderings! . . .

Darkness increased in the room. It was not very warm in there. Her hands being icy, Luce stopped her work, which Pierre was not allowed to see. They went to the window and contemplated the evening shadows across mournful fields and wooded hills. The violet forests formed a half circle against a greenish sky powdered with dust of a pale gold. A bit of the soul of Puvis de Chavannes floated there. A simple phrase of Luce made it evident that she understood how to read that subtle harmony. He was almost astonished. She was not miffed at that, and said that one might easily feel a thing that one would be incapable of expressing. Though she painted very badly, it was not altogether her fault. Through an economical turn, perhaps ill-advised, she had not finished her course at the Arts Décoratifs. Besides, poverty alone had made her turn to painting. What use in painting without a purpose? And did not Pierre think that almost all those who produce art do it without actual necessity, through vanity, in order to occupy their time, or else because at first they think they need it and later on will not confess they were mistaken? One should not be an artist save when one absolutely cannot keep to oneself the feeling one has— only when one has too much feeling. But Luce said she possessed just enough for one. She went on:

"No, for two."

(Because he made a face at her.)

The lovely golden tints in the sky began to turn to brown. The deserted plain put on a disconsolate mask. Pierre asked Luce if she was not afraid in that solitude.

"No."

"When you get home late?"

"There is no danger. The Apaches don't

come here. They have their own customs.
They are *bourgeois*, too. Besides, we have
over there an old ragpicker, and his dog.
And besides, I have no fear. Oh, I'm not
boasting about myself! I have no merit at
all in it. I am not courageous naturally.
Only, I have not as yet had any occasion
to meet with real fear. The day I do see it,
perhaps I shall be more of a poltroon than
the next one. Does one ever know what one
really is?"

"Well, I for my part know what you are,"
quoth Pierre.

"Ah, that is much easier. I myself likewise, I know . . . as to you! One
always knows better about another."

The moist chill of evening entered the
room through the closed windows. Pierre
felt a little shudder. Luce, who perceived
it at once on his neck, ran to make him a
cup of chocolate, which she heated on her
spirit-lamp. They took a bit of food. Luce
had thrown her shawl maternally over
Pierre's shoulders; and he let her do it like
a cat enjoying the warmth of the stuff.

Once more the current of their thoughts brought them back to the family history which Luce had interrupted.

Pierre continued:

"Both of you all alone, so entirely alone, you and your mother: you must be deeply attached to one another."

"Yes," said Luce. "We were very much attached."

"*Were?*" repeated Pierre.

"Oh!" said Luce, "we always love each other;" still somewhat embarrassed by the word which had escaped her without thinking. (Why must she always tell him more than she meant to? And nevertheless he did not ask, he dared not ask her. But she saw that his heart was putting the question. And it's so nice to confide in someone when one has never had the chance! The silence of the house, the half-shade of the room encouraged her to confess.) She observed:

"There's no saying or knowing what has been going on for the last four years. The whole world is changed."

"You mean to say that your mother, or that you have changed?"

"The whole world," repeated she.

"In what respect?"

"That's hard to define. One feels everywhere among people who know each other, even in the family, that the relations are not the same. One is never sure of anything any more; in the morning one says to oneself: What is it I am going to experience this night? Shall I recognize it? One is as if on a plank in the water just about to upset."

"What is it that's happened?"

"I don't know," said Luce, "I can't explain it. But it has come since the war. There is something in the air. Everybody is troubled. In families one sees people who were not capable of doing without one another marching off today, each one in his own direction. And as if intoxicated each one runs along with nose on the trail."

"Where do they go?"

"I don't know. And I believe they don't either. Either pure chance or some desire spurs them. Women take lovers. Men forget their wives. And kindly people, too, who generally appear so calm and so orderly! Everywhere we hear of households broken up. It's the same between parents and children. My mother . . ."

She stopped, then ran on:

"My mother lives her own life."

She stopped again:

"Oh, it's perfectly natural! She is still young, and poor mama has not had much happiness; she has not poured out her sum of affection. She has a right to want to make her life over again."

Pierre inquired:

"She wants to marry again?"

Luce shook her head. One could hardly know very well. . . . Pierre dared not insist.

"She loves me well, still. But it's not the way it used to be. She is able to do without me at present. . . . Poor mama! She would be so sorry if she knew that her love for me is no longer in her heart as the first of all! She would never confess that, never. . . . O, how queer it is, this life!"

She wore a sweet smile, sorrowful and roguish. Upon her hands placed on the table Pierre put his hands tenderly, and sat without motion.

"We are poor creatures," he muttered.

Luce continued in a moment:

"We two, how tranquil we are! . . . The others have the fever. The war. The factories. People are in a hurry. They hustle. To work hard, to live, to enjoy themselves . . ."

"Yes," said Pierre, "the time is short."

"All the more reason not to run!" said Luce. "One gets too soon to the end. Let us walk slowly."

"But it's time that hurries along. Hold on to it well."

"I'm holding onto it; I'm holding," said Luce, grasping his hand.

Thus back and forward, tenderly, gravely, they talked like a pair of good old friends. But they took good care that the table should stay between them.

And behold, they perceived that the night

had filled the room. Pierre rose hurriedly. Luce did nothing to retain him. The short hour had passed. They were afraid of the hour that might come. They said *au revoir* to each other with the same constraint, the same low and choked voice as when he came in. On the threshold their hands scarcely dared to press each other.

But when the door was shut, just as he was about to leave the garden, as he turned his head toward the window of the ground floor, he saw in the last gleam of the copper-colored twilight, on the pane, the outline of Luce, who was following his departure into the uncertain depths of the gleam-filled obscurity with a face full of passion. And turning back to the window, he pressed his lips against the closed pane. Their lips kissed through the wall of glass. Then Luce moved back into the shadows of the room and the curtain fell.

For the past fortnight they had been unaware of anything that was going on in the world. In Paris people might make arrests and issue condemnations as hard as they could. Germany might make treaties and tear up those she had signed. Governments might lie, the press denounce and armies kill. They did not read the papers. They knew there was the war somewhere all about them, just as there is typhus or else influenza; but that did not touch them; they did not want to think about it.

The war recalled itself to them that night. They had already gone to bed (they spent their hearts so freely in those days that when evening came they were worn out). They heard the alarm signals, each in his or her respective quarter, and declined to get up. They hid their heads in their beds under the bedclothes as a child will during a thunder-

storm—not at all from fear (they were positive that nothing could happen to them) but
in order to dream.    Listening to the air
rumbling in the night, Luce thought:

"It would be delightful to listen to the
storm as it passes, in his arms."

Pierre stopped his ears.    Let nothing
trouble his thoughts!  He insisted on pick-
ing out on the piano of memory the song of
the day passed, the melodious thread of
the hours, from the first minute that he
entered Luce's house, the slightest inflections
of her voice and her gestures, the successive
images which his eyes had hastily snapped
up—a shadow under the eyelids, a wave of
emotion that passed beneath the skin like a
shiver across the water, a smile just brushing against the lips like a sun ray, and his
palm pressed on, nestled against the nude
softness of the two extended hands—these
precious fragments that endeavored to re-
unite the magic fantasy of love in a single
close embrace.  He would not permit that
noises from without should enter there.  The
outside was for him a tiresome visitor.  The

from naked realties. And the little girl
with her precocious experience who understood the struggle for one's daily bread—
*panem quotidianum* . . . (God does not
grant it for nothing!)—revealed to her *bourgeois* friend the murderous war which, for
poor folks and particularly for women,
reigns cunningly deep and without a truce
below the lie of peace. She did not talk too
much about it, however, for fear of depress-
ing him: on seeing the excitement into which
her accounts threw him, she had an affectionate feeling of her own superiority. Like most
women she did not entertain with regard to
certain ugly facts of life the physical and
moral disgust which upset the young fellow.
There was nothing of the rebel in her. In
still worse circumstances she would have
been able to accept repugnant tasks without
repugnance and quit them quite calm and
natty, without a stain. Today she could not
do that any more, for since she had come to
know Pierre her love had caused her to be
filled with the tastes and distastes of her
friend; but that was not her fundamental

nature. Calm and smiling by reason of her
race, not pessimistic at all. Melancholy, and
the grand detached airs of life were not her
business. Life is as it is. Let us take it
as it is! It might have been worse! The
hazards of an existence which Luce had
always known to be precarious, on the look-
out for expedients—and particularly since
the war—had taught her to be careless of the
morrow. Add to this that every preoccu-
pation concerning the beyond was a stranger
to this free little French girl. Life was
enough for her. Luce found life delightful,
but it all hangs by a thread and it takes so
little to make the thread break that really
it is not worth the trouble to torment oneself about what may turn up tomorrow.
Eyes of mine, drink in the daylight that
bathes you as you pass! As to what may
come after, O, my heart, abandon yourself
in confidence to the stream! . . . And
since anyhow we can not do otherwise! . . .
And now that we love each other, isn't it
just delicious? Luce well knew that it could

not be for long.    But neither her life nor she
herself, either, would be for long.    .   .   .

She did not resemble much that little
fellow who loved her and whom she loved,
tender, ardent and nervous, happy and mis-
erable, who always enjoyed and suffered to
excess, who gave himself, who flew into a
rage, always with passion, and who was
dear to her just because he resembled her
hardly at all.    But both of them were in
accord as to a mute resolve not to look into
the future:  the girl through the carelessness
of the resigned rivulet that sings on its way
—the other through that exalted negation
which plunges into the gulf of the present
and never desires to emerge again.

THE big brother had come back again on furlough for a few days. During the first evening at home he perceived that there was something changed in the family atmosphere. What? He could not tell; but he was vexed. The mind possesses antennae which perceive at a distance before consciousness is able to touch and consider the object. And the finest of all antennae are those of vanity. Philip's agitated themselves, searched about and were surprised; they missed something. . . , Did he not have his circle of affection which rendered unto him the customary homage—the attentive audience to which in miserly fashion he doled out his stories—his parents who brooded him under their touched admiration—the young brother? . . . Stop there! It was he, exactly he who was missing to the appeal.

He was present of course but he did not
exert himself about his big brother; he did
not beg for confidences as was his wont,
which the other used to take pleasure in
denying. Pitiful vanity! Philip, who on
former occasions affected in regard of the
ardent questions of his younger brother a
sort of protective and bantering lacka-
daisicalness, was hurt that he did not put
them this time. It was he who tried to pro-
voke them: he became more loquacious and
he looked at Pierre as if he wished him to
feel that his talk was meant for him. At
another time Pierre would have thrilled with
joy and caught on the fly the handkerchief
that was tossed him. But he quietly permitted Philip to pick it up for himself if
he had any desire to do so. Philip, feeling
piqued, tried irony. Instead of being
troubled, Pierre answered with composure
in the same detached tone. Philip wanted
to discuss, became agitated, harangued.
After a few minutes he found that he was
haranguing all by himself. Pierre looked
on at his efforts wearing an air of saying:

"Go ahead, my dear boy! If that is any pleasure to you! Continue! I'm listening. . . ."

That insolent little smile! . . . Their rôles were reversed.

Philip stopped talking, much mortified, and observed his young brother more attentively, who, however, did not occupy himself further with him. How he had changed! The parents, who saw him every day, had not noticed anything; but the penetrating and moreover jealous eyes of Philip did not find any more the well known expression after several months of absence. Pierre had a happy, languid, thoughtless, torpid air, indifferent as to persons, inattentive to what is about them, floating in an atmosphere of voluptuous dream, like a young girl. And Philip felt that he counted for nothing in the little brother's thoughts.

Since he was no less expert in analyzing himself than in observing others, he was quick to recover consciousness of his own vexation and laugh at it. Vanity thrust aside, he interested himself in Pierre and

searched for the secret of his metamorphosis.
He would have liked well to have solicited
his confidence, but that was a business to
which he was not habituated, and besides,
little brother did not seem to have any need
of confiding; with a careless and chaffing
unconstraint he looked on while Philip
attempted awkwardly to spread the net; and
with his hands in his pockets, smiling, his
thoughts elsewhere, whistling a little air, he
answered vaguely, without listening carefully
to what he was being asked—then, all of a
sudden, turned off to his own regions.  Good
night!   And he was no longer there.   One
caught only at his reflection in the water,
which escaped from between one's fingers.—
And Philip, like a lover disdained, felt all
his value now and experienced the attraction
of the mystery in this heart which he had
lost.

The key to the enigma came to him by
pure chance.  As he was coming home in
the evening by Boulevard Montparnasse, in
the dark he passed Pierre and Luce.  He
was afraid they might have noticed him.

But they cared little for what surrounded them. Closely pressed together, Pierre supporting his arm on the arm of Luce and holding her hand with fingers interlaced, they strolled along with short steps immersed in the hungry and gluttonous tenderness of Eros and Psyche as they lie at length on the nuptial couch in the Farnesina. The close embrace of their gaze fused them into a single being like a waxen group. Philip, leaning against a tree, looked upon them as they passed, stopped, went on and disappeared in the dark. And his heart was full of pity for the two children. He thought:

"My life is sacrificed. So be it! But it is not right to take those also. If at the least I could pay for their happiness!"

The next morning, in spite of his polite inattention, Pierre noticed vaguely—in actual fact not at once, but after some reflection—the affectionate tone of his brother with him. And, getting half awake, he perceived his kind eyes which he had not noticed before. Philip looked at him with such clarity that Pierre had an impression that this gaze was scrutinizing him; and awkwardly he hastened at once to push the shutter over his secret. But Philip smiled, rose, and putting his hand on his shoulder proposed that they should take a turn in the open. Pierre could not resist the new confidence which was tendered him and together they proceeded to the Luxembourg near at hand. The big brother had kept his hand on the shoulder of the younger and the latter felt himself proud of the re-established accord. His tongue was loosed. They talked animatedly of intellectual things, of books, their reflections on men, their new experiences—of everything except the subject both were thinking about. It was like a tacit convention. They were happy to feel themselves intimate, with a secret between them. While chatting Pierre inquired of himself:

"Does he know? But how could he know?"

Philip observed him as he chattered along and kept on smiling. Pierre ended by stopping short in the midst of a sentence.

"What's the matter with you?"

"Nothing.   I'm just looking at you.   I am delighted with you."

They shook hands.   While they were returning Philip said:

"Are you happy?"

Without speaking Pierre nodded with his head—yes.

"You are right, my boy.   A great, beautiful thing is happiness.   Take my portion . . ."

In order not to trouble him, Philip during his furlough avoided making any allusion to the near incorporation of Pierre's class in the army.   But on the day of his departure he could not prevent himself from expressing his anxiety at seeing his young brother exposed very soon to the trials which he knew only too well.   Scarcely did a shadow cross the brow of the young lover.   He drew his eyebrows a bit together, blinked with his eyes as if to drive off a troublesome vision, and said:

"Enough!   Later on!   *Chi lo sa?*"

"We know it only too well," said Philip.

"What in any case I do know," said

Pierre, vexed that he should insist, "is that when I am down there I for my part shall do no killing."

Without contradicting him, Philip smiled sorrowfully, knowing well what the implacable power of the crowd does with weak souls and with their will.

MARCH was back again with a longer day
and the first songs of birds. But along with
the days increased the sinister flames of the
war. The air was feverish with waiting
for springtime—and waiting for the cata-
clysm. One heard the monstrous rumbling
grow in intensity, the arms of millions of
enemies clashing together, heaped up for the
past months against the dyke of the trenches,
and all ready to spill over like a tidal bore
upon the Ile de France and the nave of La
Cité. The shadow of frightful rumors
preceded the plague; a fantastic report of
poisoned gases, of deadly venom scattered
through the air, which was about, so it was
said, to descend on whole provinces and
destroy everything like the asphyxiating
overflow from Pelée Mountain. Finally the
visits of bombing Gothas, coming oftener

and oftener, cleverly kept up the nervousness
of Paris.

Pierre and Luce continued to refuse to
recognize anything about them, but the slow
fever which they breathed in, whether they
would or not, from that atmosphere heavy
with menace, kindled the desire that glowed
in their young bodies.    Three years of war
had propagated in European souls a freedom of morals which reached even the most
honest and straight.    And of the two children, neither one nor the other, had any
religious beliefs.    But they were protected
by their delicacy of heart, their instinctive
modesty.    Only, in secret they had decided to
give themselves completely one to the other
before the blind cruelty of mankind should
separate them.    They had not spoken of this.
They said it to themselves that evening.

Once or twice during the week Luce's
mother was kept at the factory by her night
work.    On these nights Luce, in order not
to stay alone in that desert quarter, slept in
Paris with a girl friend.    Nobody kept
watch over her.    The two lovers took advan-

tage of this freedom to pass a portion of the evening together and sometimes they took a simple dinner in a little out-of-the-way restaurant. On leaving after dinner on this mid-March evening they heard the bomb-alert signal sound. They took refuge in the nearest place as if it were an affair of a rain shower, and for some time amused themselves observing their chance comrades. But the danger seeming distant or no longer there, although nothing had occurred to announce the end of the bomb-warning, Luce and Pierre, who did not want to get home too late, went on their way chatting gaily. They followed an old dark and narrow street near Saint Sulpice. They had just passed a hackney coach standing idle, both horse and driver asleep, near the gate of a *porte cochère*. They were twenty steps away and on the other sidewalk, when everything about them shuddered: a red, blinding flash, a roll of thunder, a rain of loosened tiles and broken windowpanes! Near the buttress of a house which made a sharp projection into the street they flattened

themselves against the wall and their bodies
interlaced. . By the gleam of the explosion
they had seen their own eyes full of love and
dismay. And when the darkness fell again
Luce's voice was saying:

"No, Pierre. I want no more."

And Pierre felt upon his own lips the lips
and the teeth of the passionate girl. They
remained palpitating in the darkness of the
street. Some paces away some men, issuing
from the houses, picked the dying coachman
from among the remnants of the smashed
vehicle; they passed quite close to them with
the unfortunate man whose blood was falling
drop by drop. Luce and Pierre remained
petrified; so closely knit together that when
consciousness revived in them it seemed as
if their bodies had been naked in the pressure. They loosened their hands and lips
grown together which drank of the loved one
like roots. And, both of them, they began
to tremble.

"Let us go home!" said Luce, invaded by
a sacred terror.

She dragged him away.

"Luce! you will not let me leave this life before . . . ?"

"Oh, God," said Luce, squeezing his arm, "that thought would be worse than death!"

"My love, my love!" they kept repeating, one to the other.

Once more they came to a stop.

"When shall I be yours?" said Pierre.

(He could not have dared to ask: "When shall you be mine?")

Luce noticed this and was touched by it.

"Adored one," she said to him, ". . . very soon! Let's not hurry. You can not desire it more than I wish it! . . . Let us stay this way a little while. . . . It is splendid! . . . This month longer, right to the end! . . ."

"Until Easter?" he murmured.

(This year Easter was the last day in March.)

"Yes, at the Resurrection."

"Ah," quoth he, "there's the Death before Resurrection."

"Hush!" she interposed, closing his mouth with her own.

They drew away from each other.

"This night, it's our betrothal," whispered Pierre.

Huddled against each other while they walked in the shadows, they wept gently with tenderness. The ground crackled underfoot with the broken glass and the sidewalk was bloody. Death and the night were lying in ambush round about their love. But above their heads like a magic circle beyond the embrasure of the two black walls in the narrow street, as through a chimney, the heart of a star throbbed against the deep pulpy grain of the sky. . . .

Lo and behold! The voices of the bells sing out, lights are rekindled and the streets are animate once more. The air is free of foes. Paris breathes again. Death has flown.

THEY had come to the day preceding Palm Sunday. Every day they saw each other for hours together; and they did not even try to hide themselves any more. They no longer had any accounts to render the world. By such gossamer threads were they attached to it and so near to breaking!—Two days before, the German grand offensive had been started. The wave advanced along a front of nearly a hundred kilometers. Fast following emotions caused the City to vibrate: the explosion of Courneuve, which had shaken Paris like an earthquake; the incessant air bomb-alarms which broke in on sleep and wore out nerves. And on this morning of Saturday after a troubled night all those who were not able to close an eyelid until very late were roused again by the thunder of the mysterious cannon buried in the far distance, which, beyond the Somme,

launched death in trial shots, as if from
another planet.    In the course of the earlier
shots, which were attributed to the coming
back of the aerial Gothas, people had taken
refuge in a docile way inside their cellars;
but a danger that continues becomes in time
a habit to which life accommodates itself;
and the peril is not far from turning out an
attraction even, when the risks run are common to all and are not too great.    Besides,
the weather was too lovely; it was a pity to
bury one's self alive: before noon all the
world was out of doors; and the streets and
gardens, the terraces of the cafés had a
festival air on this radiant and burning
afternoon.

It was this afternoon Pierre and Luce had
selected to pass, far from the crowd, in the
forest of Chaville.    For the past ten days
they had existed in an uplifted calm.    Profound peace at the heart, and nerves on edge.
They had a feeling like existing on an islet,
about which rushed a frantic current: a
vertigo of sight and hearing carried them
away.    But with eyelids lowered and hands

on ears, when the bolt is pushed on the door,
suddenly in one's inner deep there comes a
silence, a blinding silence, the moveless
summer day, when Joy invisible like a hidden bird sings its song, fresh and liquid,
like a brook. O Joy! magical singer,
warblings of happiness! I know too well it
suffices that a slit should open between my
lids or that my finger should cease to push a
moment against my ear, and the foam and
roar of the stream will follow in. Frail
dyke! Just to know it so frail exalts the
mood of Joy which I know is threatened.
Peace and silence itself take on a passionate
look! . . .

The woods once reached, they held each
other by the hand. The first days of spring
are a new wine that rises to the head. The
youthful sun intoxicates with the purest juice
of its vine. Light still floats over the leafless wood, and athwart the bare branches the
blue eye of the sky fascinates the reason and
lulls it to sleep. . . . Scarcely did they
endeavor to exchange a few words. Their
tongues declined to finish a phrase once

started.    Their legs were weak and they
hated to walk.    Under the sunshine and the
silence of the woods they tottered.    The earth
drew them.    Just to lie down in the path!
Just to let themselves be carried along on the
rim of the colossal wheel of the worlds. . . .

They scrambled over the bank of the way-
side, entered a thicket and, side by side on
the old dead leaves through which violets
showed their buds, they stretched themselves
out.    The first songs of the birds and the
distant thuds of the guns mingled with the
village bells that were proclaiming the
festival of the morrow.    The luminous air
vibrated hope, faith, love, death.    Notwith-
standing the solitude they spoke in whispers.
Their hearts were oppressed: by happiness?
or by sorrow?    They could not have told.
They were submerged in their dream.
Lucile, immobile, stretched out, her arms
close to her body, her eyes open, absorbed
and gazing at the sky, felt rising in her a
hidden suffering which since the morning she
forced herself to drive away in order not to
mar the joy of the holiday.    Pierre laid his

head on Luce's knees in the hollow of her
skirt like a child who goes to sleep with its
face close couched against the warmth of
the stomach.   And Luce without a word
caressed with her hands the ears and eyes,
the nose and lips of her beloved one.   Dear
spiritual hands which seemed, as in the tales
about fairies, to have little mouths at the
finger-tips!   And Pierre, a thinking piano,
divined the meaning of the little waves that
sped under the tips, the emotions that passed
through the soul of his darling.   He heard
her sigh before she had begun to sigh.   Luce
had raised herself with her body leaning
forward and, with breathing oppressed, she
moaned in a whisper:

"Pierre, oh, Pierre!"

Pierre looked at her troubled.

"Oh, Pierre!  What are we, anyway? . . .
What is it they want of us? . . .  What do
we want? . . .  What is this going on within
us?  These guns, these birds, this war, this
love. . . .  These hands, body, eyes. . . .
Where am I? . . .  and what am I?"

Pierre, who did not recognize this expres-

sion of bewilderment in her, wanted to take
her in his arms.    But she repulsed him.

"No! No!"

And hiding her face in her hands she
thrust face and hands together into the grass.
Pierre was upset and begged of her:

"Luce!  .  .  ."

He thrust his head close to that of Luce.

"Luce," he repeated, "what's the matter
with you?    Is it against me?"

She raised her head.

"No!"

And he saw tears in her eyes.

"Are you in trouble?"

"Yes."

"Why?"

"I don't know."

"Tell me  .  .  ."

"Ah, I'm ashamed," she said.  .  .  .

"Ashamed?    About what?"

"About everything."

She fell silent.

Since the morning she had been haunted
by a sorrowful memory, painful and degrad-
ing;  her mother, crazed by the poison that

crept about in the promiscuous conditions of
the factories made for luxury and for murder,
in those human vats, no longer kept up any
restraint upon herself.  At home she had
indulged in a scene of furious jealousy with
her lover, without caring if her daughter
heard; and Luce had learned that her
mother was with child.  For her this was
like a blot that extended to herself, whose
entire love, whose love for Pierre was pol-
luted thereby.  That is why when Pierre had
approached her she had repulsed him; she
was ashamed of herself and of him. . . .
Ashamed of him?  Poor Pierre! . . .

He remained there, humiliated, and not
daring to budge any more.  She was struck
with remorse, smiled in the midst of tears
and, resting her head on Pierre's knees, said:

"It is my turn!"

Still disquieted, Pierre smoothed her hair
as one pets a cat.  He murmured:

"Luce, what is all this?  Tell me . . ."

"Nothing," she responded.  "I've seen
sorrowful things."

He had too much respect for her secrets to

insist.    But Luce went on a few minutes later:

"Ah, there are moments  .  .  .  One is ashamed to belong to mankind."

Pierre trembled.

"Yes," said he.

And after a silence, bending over, he said very low:

"Forgive me!"

Luce sprang up impetuously, threw herself on Pierre's neck, repeating:

"Forgive me!"

And their mouths found each other.

The two children felt the need of consoling one another, both of them.    Without saying it aloud they were thnking:

"Luckily we are going to die!    The most frightful thing would be to become one of those men who are proud of being man—to destroy, to render vile  .  .  ."

Lips touching lips, eyelashes brushing eyelashes, they plunged their gaze one in the other, smiling and with a tender pity.    They did not tire of that divine sentiment which is the purest form of love.    At last they tore themselves from their contemplation and Luce, with eyes again serene, perceived once more the gentle hue of the sky, the sweetness of the renewing trees and the breath of flowers.

"How lovely it all is!" she exclaimed.

She was thinking:

"Why are things so beautiful?   And we so poor, so mediocre, so ugly!   (unless it be you, my love, unless it be you!)   . . ."

She gazed at Pierre again:

"Pshaw!   What are others to me?"

And with the magnificent illogicality of love she burst out laughing, sprang up with a leap, rushed into the wood and cried: "Catch me, catch me!"

They played like two children all the rest of the day.   And when they were very tired they returned with slow steps toward the valley filled like a basket with the sheaves of the setting sun.   Everything they savored seemed new to them—with one heart for two, with two bodies for one.

THEY were five friends about the same age, met together at the house of one of them, five young comrades at their studies whom a certain conformity of mind and a first sorting out of opinions had grouped together apart from the rest. And yet no two of them who thought the same way. Beneath the pretended unanimity of forty millions of Frenchmen there are forty million brains that keep right to themselves. Thought in France is like the country, a state composed of small properties. From one bit of farm to the other the five friends tried to exchange their ideas across the hedge. But they did that only to affirm themselves more imperatively in their several opinions, each for himself. Each one, for that matter, liberal in mind, and, if not all of them republicans, all foes of intellectual or social reaction, or any backward return.

110

Jacques Sée was the most blazingly in favor of the war. This generous young Jew had espoused all the passions the spirit of France contained. All through Europe his cousins in Israel espoused like him the causes and the ideas of their adopted countries. Moreover, according to their method, they even had a tendency toward an exaggeration of whatever they adopted. This fine fellow, with ardent but rather heavy voice and look, with his regular features as if marked with a stamp imposed, was more pronounced in his convictions than was needful, and violent in contradiction. According to him, all that was necessary was a crusade made by the democracies to deliver the nations and extinguish war. Four years of the philanthropic slaughterhouse had not convinced him. He was one of those who will never accept the flat contradiction of facts. He had a twofold pride, the secret pride of his race, which race he wished to rehabilitate, and his pride personal that wanted to prove itself right. He wished this all the more because he was not entirely sure of it. His sincere idealism served as a screen against exacting instincts too long suppressed and to a need for action and adventure, which was no less sincere.

Antoine Naudé, he too, was for the war. But that was because he could not do otherwise. This big honest young *bourgeois,* with his rosy cheeks, placid and keen, who had a short breath and rolled his *r* with the pretty grace of the provinces of the Centre, contemplated with a quiet smile the enthusiastic transports of his friend Sée; or else he knew how on occasion to make him climb a tree with a careless word;—but the big, lazy fellow took precious care not to follow him up! What is the use of getting in a sweat for or against what does not depend upon ourselves? It is only in the tragedies that one finds the heroic and loquacious conflict between duty and one's pleasure. When we have no choice, we do our duty without wasting words. It was no jollier on that account. Naudé neither admired nor recriminated. His good sense told him that, once the train started and the war in motion, it was necessary to roll along with it; there was no other

position to take.    As for searching after the
responsibilities, that was merely time lost.
When I am forced to fight it gives me a gay
outlook, a pretty consolation, to know that I
might have not fought—if things had really
been  .  .  .  what they haven't been!

The responsibilities?    Now for Bernard
Saisset they were exactly the primordial
question; he was obstinate in disentangling
that knot of snakes; or rather, like a little
Fury, he brandished the snakes above his
head.    A frail boy, distinguished looking,
impassioned, too many nerves, burning with
a too lively sensitiveness of the brain, belonging to the wealthy *bourgeoisie* and an
old republican family which had played a
part in the highest offices of State, he pro-
fessed, through reaction, all the ultra-revolu-
tionary passions.    He had inspected too near
at hand the masters of the day and what they
brought forth.    He accused all the governments—and by preference his own.    He
talked of nothing any more but of syndical-
ists and bolsheviki; he had just made a dis-
covery of them and he fraternized with them,

as if he had known them from infancy.
Without knowing too well which, he saw no
remedy save in a total upset of society.   He
hated war; but he would have sacrificed
himself with joy in a war between classes—
a war against his own class, a war against
himself.

The fourth in the group, Claude Puget,
sat by at these jousts of words with a cold
and somewhat disdainful attention.   Coming from the very undermost *bourgeoisie,*
poor, uprooted from his province by a passing inspector of schools who remarked his
intelligence, prematurely deprived of the
intimate influence of his family, this winner
of a *Lycée* scholarship, accustomed to depend
upon himself alone, to live only with himself, merely lived by himself and for himself.   An egotistic philosopher given to
analysis of the soul, voluptuously immersed
in his introspection like a big cat curled up
in a ball, he was not moved at all by the
agitation of the others.   These three friends
of his who never could agree among themselves he put in the same bag—with the

"populars." Did not all three forfeit their
social rank by wishing to partake in the
aspirations of the mob? Truth to say, the
mob was a different crowd for each of them.
But for Puget the crowd, whatever it might
be, was always wrong. The crowd was the
enemy. The intellect should remain alone
and follow its particular laws and found,
apart from the vulgar crowd and the State,
the small and closed kingdom of thought.

And Pierre, seated near the window, dis-
tractedly looked out of doors, and dreamed.
Generally speaking, he mingled in these
juvenile assaults with passion. But today
it seemed to him a humming of idle words
which he listened to from so far away, oh,
so far away! in a bored and mocking demi-
torpidity. Plunged in their discussions, the
others were a long while in remarking his
muteness. But at last Saisset, accustomed
to find in Pierre an echo of his verbal
bolshevisms, was astonished at failing to
hear it reverberate any more and put the
question to him.

Pierre waked up in a hurry, reddened, smiled and asked:

"What were you talking about?"

They were most indignant.

"Why, you haven't been listening to anything!"

"What, then, were you brooding about?" asked Naudé.

A little confused, a little impertinent, Pierre replied:

"About the springtide.  It has come back all right without your permission.  It will clear out without our help."

All of them crushed him with their disdain.  Naudé taunted him as a "poet." And Jacques Sée as a *poseur*.

Puget alone fixed his eyes on him with curiosity and irony in them, his wrinkled eyes with their cold pupils.

"Flying ant!"

"What?" questioned Pierre, rather amused.

"Beware of the wings!" said Puget.  "It's the nuptial flight.  It only lasts one hour."

"Life does not last much more," said Pierre.

DURING Passion Week they saw one another every day. Pierre went to see Luce in her isolated house. The thin and hungry garden was waking up. They passed the afternoon there. They felt now an antipathy toward Paris and the crowd, against life also. At certain moments even, a moral paralysis kept them silent, immovable, one close to the other, without a wish to stir. A strange feeling was at work in both of them. They were afraid! Fear—in the measure that the day approached when they should give themselves the one to the other—fear through excess of love, through the purification of soul which the ugly things, the cruelties, the shameful facts of life frightened, and which, in an intoxication of passion and melancholy, dreamed of being delivered from it all. . . . They said nothing about it to each other.

The most of their time they passed in

babbling gently about their future lodgings, their work in common, their little household. They arranged in advance, down to the smallest item of their installation, the furniture, the wall papers, the spot for each object. A true woman, the evocation of these tender nothings, intimate and familiar images of daily life, moved Luce sometimes to tears. They tasted the exquisite small joys of the hearth of the future. . . . They knew that nothing of that sort would occur—Pierre through the presentiment of his native pessimism—Luce through the clairvoyance of love which understood the practical impossibility of the marriage. . . . That is why they hasted to enjoy it in their dream. And each concealed from the other the certainty felt that it would not be anything else but a dream. Each one believed that this secret was personal and watched, deeply touched, over the other's illusion.

When they had exhausted the mournful delights of the impossible future they were overcome with fatigue, as if they had lived through all of it. Then they rested them-

selves, seated under the arbor with the dried-
up vines, while the sun melted the congealed
sap; and, Pierre's head on Luce's shoulder,
they listened dreamily to the humming of the
earth.    Behind the passing clouds the young
sun of March played bo-peep, laughed and
disappeared.    Clear sunrays, somber shadows ran across the plain as in a soul run
joys and sorrows.

"Luce," said Pierre abruptly, "don't you
recollect? . . . It was long, long ago. . . .
Even then we were like this. . . ."

"Yes," said Luce, "that's true. All of it,
I remember all. . . . But where were
we? . . ."

They amused themselves by trying to recall
under what shapes they had known one
another before.    Already as human beings?
Perhaps.    But certainly at that time Pierre
was the girl and Luce the lover. . . . Birds
in the air?    When she was a small child her
mother told Luce that she had been a little
wild goose that had fallen down the chimney; ah! she had thoroughly broken her
wings! . . . But where particularly they

enjoyed finding themselves again was in the
elementary fluid forms that penetrate one
another, twist about and untwist like the
volutes of a dream or else of smoke: white
clouds that dissolve in the gulf of the sky,
little waves that play about, the rain on the
soil, the dew on the bush, seeds of dandelion
that swim at the beck of the air. . . . But
the wind carries them away. Provided it
does not begin to blow again and that we
shall not lose each other any more for all
eternity! . . .

But he decided:

"As for me, I believe that we never did
quit one another; we were together just as
we are now, lying against each other; only,
we were asleep and we dreamed dreams.
From time to time we awake. . . . With
difficulty. . . . I feel your breath, your
cheek against mine. . . . One makes a
great effort; we bring our mouths together.
. . . One falls back asleep. . . . Darling, darling, I am here, I hold your hand,
don't let me go! . . . Now it is not quite

yet the hour, spring hardly shows the end of his icy nose. . . ."

"Like yours," said Luce.

"Very soon we shall awake on a fine summer's day. . . ."

"We ourselves shall be that fine day of summer," says Luce.

"The warm shade of the limetrees, the sun through the branches, the bees that sing. . . ."

"The peach on the warm wall and its perfumed pulp. . . ."

"The noon spell of the harvesters and their golden sheaves. . . ."

"The lazy cattle that chew their cud. . . ."

"And at evensong, by the sunset like a flowerset pool, the liquid light that runs across the tops of the fields. . . ."

"Yes, we shall be everything," quoth Luce, "everything that is good and sweet to see and to have, to kiss and to eat, to touch and inhale. . . . What's left over we shall leave to them," she added, pointing to the city and its smoke wreaths.

She laughed. Then, kissing her friend, she said:

"We have chanted our little duet well. What do you say, my friend Pierrot?"

"Yea, verily, Jessica," he replied.

"My poor Pierrot," she returned, "we are none too well equipped for this world, where people know how to sing nothing else but the *Marseillaise!* . . ."

"Good enough if they even knew how to sing that!"

"We have got off at the wrong station, we left the train too early."

"I'm afraid," said Pierre, "that the next station would have been still worse. Can you see us, my darling, in the social fabric of the future—the hive they promise us, where none will have the right to live except for the queen bee's service or for the republic?"

"Laying eggs from morning to night like a *mitrailleuse* or from morning to night licking the eggs of others. . . . Thank you for that choice!" said Luce.

"Oh, Luce, little ugly one, how ugly you talk," said Pierre laughing.

"Yes, it's very bad, I know it.    I am good for nothing.    Nor you either, my friend. You are just as ill fitted for killing or maiming men as I am for sewing them up again, like those wretched horses when they are ripped up at the bullfights, so that they can serve again at the next affray.    We two are useless beings and dangerous, who have the ridiculous, criminal pretention to live only in order to love those we do love, likewise my little lover lad and my friends, honest people and little children, the good light of the day, also good white bread and everything that is pretty and right for me to put in my mouth. It's shameful, it's shameful!    Blush for me, Pierrot!  . . .    But we shall be well punished!    There is going to be no place for us in that factory of the State, without rest and without truce, which the earth will be soon. . . . Luckily we shall not be here!"

"Yes, what happiness!" quoth Pierre.

*"If in thine arms, O Lady of my heart,*
  *I die, to greater fame I'll not aspire,*
  *Content upon thy bosom to expire*
*Whilst kissing thee and thus from living part. . . ."*

"Well, little darling, what sort of a fashion is that?"

"Nevertheless it is after a good old French mode. It's by Ronsard," said Pierre:

*". . . else I would only claim*
*A century hence, sans glory and sans fame*
*Slothful to die upon thy lap, Cassandra. . . ."*

"A hundred years!" sighed Luce. "He doesn't ask much! . . ."

*"Or I mistake, or more delights are heaped*
*In death like that than all the honors reaped*
*By Caesar great or firebolt Alexander."*

"Naughty, naughty, naughty little scamp! have you no shame? In this epoch of heroes!"

"There are too many," said Pierre. "I would rather be a little fellow who loves, a babe of a man."

"The babe of a woman who still has on his lips the milk from my breast," cried Luce, seizing him round the neck. "My babe, my own!"

SURVIVORS of those days who, since then, have been witness to the dazzling change of fortune, will have forgotten doubtless the menacing heavy flight of the dark wing which, during that week, covered the Isle de France and touched Paris with its shadow. Joy does not take further stock in past trials.—The German drive reached the line of its summit between Holy Monday and Holy Wednesday. The Somme traversed, Bapaume, Vesle, Guiscard, Roye, Noyon, Albert carried. Eleven hundred guns taken. Sixty thousand prisoners. . . . Symbol of the land of grace trampled upon, on Holy Tuesday died Debussy the harmonious. A lyre that is snapped. . . . "Poor little expiring Greece!" What will remain of it? A few chiseled vases, a few perfect stelae which the grass will invade from the

Path of Tombs.    Immortal vestiges of
ruined Athens. . . .

As from the height of a hill, Pierre and
Luce watched the shadow that moved upon
the town.    Still wrapped in the rays of their
love, they waited without fear for the end of
the brief day.    Now they would be two in
the night.    Like to the evening *Angelus*
there rose up to them, conjured up, the voluptuous melancholy of the lovely chords of
Debussy which they had so greatly loved.
More than it had ever done in any other
time, music responded to the need of their
hearts.    Music was the only art which rendered the voice of the delivered soul behind
the screen of forms.

On Holy Thursday they walked, Luce on
Pierre's arm and holding his hand, along the
streets of the suburb, soused with the rain.
Gusts of wind scurried over the moistened
plain.    They noted neither rain nor wind,
neither the hideousness of the fields nor the
muddy ways.    They seated themselves on
the low wall of a park, a section of which
had recently fallen in.    Under Pierre's

umbrella, which scarcely protected her head and shoulders, Luce, her legs hanging down and her hands wet, her rubber coat all steeped, looked at the water dripping down. When the wind stirred the branches a little fire of drops sounded "clop, clop!" Luce was silent, smiling, tranquilly luminous. A profound joy bathed them.

"Why does one love so much?" said Pierre.

"Ah, Pierre, you do not love me so very much if you ask that."

"I ask you that," said Pierre, "in order to make you say what I know just as well as you."

"You want me to give you some compliments. But you'll be neatly caught. For if you know why I love you, I for my part do not know why."

"You don't know?" said Pierre in consternation.

"Why no!" (She was laughing in her sleeve.) "And there is no need at all why I should know. When one asks why something is, it means that one is not sure about it, that the thing is not good.  Now that I do love, no more why!  No more where or when or for, nor how either!  My love is, my love is!  All beside may exist if it cares to."

Their faces kissed each other.  The rain took advantage of that, gliding under the awkward umbrella in order to brush with its fingers their hair and cheeks; between their lips they drank in a little cold drop.

Pierre remarked:

"But the others?"

"What others?" quoth Luce.

"The poor," answered Pierre.  "All those who are not us?"

"Let them do as we do!  Let them love!"

"And be loved?  Luce, all the world can not do that."

"Why, yes!"

"Why, no.  You don't realize the value of the gift you have made me."

"To give one's heart to love, one's lips to the beloved is to give one's eyes to the light; it isn't giving, it's taking."

"There are blind people."

"We cannot cure them, Pierrot. Let's do the seeing for them!"

Pierre remained silent.

"What are you thinking of?" asked she.

"I am thinking that on this day, very far from us, very near, He suffered the Passion, He who came on earth to cure the blind."

Luce took his hand:

"Do you believe in Him?"

"No, Luce, I believe no longer. But he remains always the friend of those he has accepted, even once, at his table. And you, do you know him?"

"Hardly," responded Luce. "They never talked to me about him. But without knowing him I love him. . . . For I know that he loved."

"Not as we do."

"Why not? We ourselves have a poor little heart that knows only how to love you, my love. But He; He loved all of us. But it's always the same love."

"Would you like we should go tomorrow," asked Pierre, much moved, "in honor of His death? . . . I was told that they will have fine music at Saint Gervais!"

"Yes, I would love well to go to church with you on that day. I am sure He will give us welcome. And being nearer to Him, one is nearer each to the other.

They fell silent. . . . Rain, rain, rain. The rain falls. The night falls.

"At this hour tomorrow," said she, "we shall be down there."

The fog was penetrating. She gave a little shudder.

"Darling, you are not cold?" he asked, disquieted.

She rose:

"No, no. Everything is love to me. I love everything and everything loves me. The rain loves me, the wind loves me, the gray sky and the cold—and my little greatly beloved. . . ."

For Holy Friday the heavens remained clothed in their long gray veils; but the air was soft and calm. In the streets one saw flowers, jonquils, stocks. Pierre took a few which she kept in her hand. They followed the peaceful Quai des Orfèvres and passed along the base of pure Notre-Dame. The charm of the Old City, clothed in a discreet light, surrounded them with its noble gentleness. On the Place Saint Gervais pigeons flew up under their feet. They followed them with their eyes about the façade of the church; one of the birds settled on the head of a statue. At the top of the steps to the *parvis* before the church, as they were about to enter, Luce turned about and perceived in the midst of the crowd a few steps away a little girl with reddish hair, about a dozen years old, leaning against the portal, both arms raised above her head, who was look-

ing at them. She had the fine and somewhat archaic face of some little cathedral
statue, with an enigmatic smile, graceful,
shrewd and tender. Luce smiled also at her
while calling Pierre's attention to her. But
the little girl's gaze passed over her head
and suddenly changed to fright. And
hiding her face in her hands the child
vanished.

"What is the matter with her?" asked
Luce.

But Pierre did not look.

They entered. Above their heads the
dove was cooing. Last noise from outside.
The voices of Paris were quenched. The
fresh air ceased. The hangings of the
organ, the lofty vaultings, the curtain of
stones and sounds parted them from the
world.

They installed themselves in one of the
side aisles between the second and the third
chapel on the left as you enter. In the
hollow of a pier both of them crouched,
seated on some steps, hidden from the rest
of the assembly. Turning their backs to

the choir, on raising their eyes they saw the summit of the altar, the crucifix and the stained windows of a lateral chapel. The beautiful old chants wept out their pious melancholy. They were holding hands, the two little pagans, before the Great Friend, in the church all swathed in mourning. And both of them at the same time murmured in a low voice:

"Great Friend, before your face I take him, I take her. Unite us! You see our hearts."

And their fingers remained joined and interlaced like the straw of a basket. They were one single flesh which the waves of music passed through with their shivering notes. They took to dreaming, as if they lay in the same bed.

Luce saw again in her thought that little girl with reddish hair. And behold it seemed to her that she recalled how she had seen her before in a dream the past night. She could not reach the point of knowing whether that was actually true, or if she were projecting the vision of the present back to the past slumber. Then, weary of the effort, her thoughts allowed themselves to float.

Pierre pondered over the days of his short, expended life. The lark that rises from the misty plain to reach the sun . . . How far it is! How high it is! Will it ever be reached? . . . The fog thickens. There is no earth any more, there are no heavens any more. And strength gives out . . . Suddenly, while beneath the vault of the choir a Gregorian *vocalise* trickled down, the jubilant song gushed forth, and out from the shadows emerges the little shivering form of the lark that swims on the sea of light without shore. . . .

A pressure of their fingers recalled to them that they were swimming together. They found themselves again in the darkness of the church, closely pressed together, listening to the beautiful chants; their hearts melted with love and touched the summits of the purest joy. And both of them desired —they prayed—never to descend to earth again.

At that moment Luce, who had just kissed her dear little comrade with a passionate glance—(his eyes half closed and his lips parted, he appeared lost in an ecstasy of happiness and raised his head in a rush of thankful joy toward that supreme Power which we look for instinctively on high)— Luce saw with terror, in the red and gilded window of the chapel, the face of the reddish-haired child of the *parvis* who was smiling at her. And as she sat mute, frozen with astonishment, she saw once more on that strange visage the same expression of fright and of pity.

And at the same instant the great pier against which they leaned their backs moved, and down to its very base the entire church trembled. And Luce, whose heart beats deadened in her the crash of the explosion and the shrieks of the crowd, threw herself without having time to fear or to suffer upon Pierre, in order to cover him with her body like a hen with her brood— upon Pierre, who with closed eyes was smiling with happiness. With a maternal movement she clasped the dear head against her bosom and that with all her power; and, coiled upon him, her mouth on his neck, they shrank together to their utmost.

And the massive pier crumbled down upon them with one crash.

THE END